THREE MEN IN A BOAT

This is not one of those Great Travel books: it does not describe sailing across the world's dangerous seas or a brave journey up the Amazon river. It is only a small journey, in a small boat. But it is still an adventure – an adventure that you or I or anyone could experience . . . and tell stories about afterwards.

Who are the heroes of this journey? They are George, Harris, and 'J' (and of course, Montmorency the dog): three young men that we could meet anywhere, in any century. They fall in the river and lose things, they argue and laugh, and tell each other stories. They are full of exciting plans and enthusiasm, but they can't get out of bed in the morning. They want to be great adventurers, but actually, when it rains, they would prefer to be in comfortable chairs in front of a warm fire.

Do our heroes enjoy their adventures on the river? Do they ever learn to cook eggs over a camp fire, or to open a tin without a tin-opener? But this is their story: the story of three men – and the dog – in a boat.

OXFORD BOOKWORMS LIBRARY
Human Interest

Three Men in a Boat

Stage 4 (1400 headwords)

Series Editor: Jennifer Bassett
Founder Editor: Tricia Hedge
Activities Editors: Jennifer Bassett and Alison Baxter

JEROME K. JEROME

Three Men in a Boat

Retold by
Diane Mowat

OXFORD UNIVERSITY PRESS

2000

Oxford University Press,
Great Clarendon Street, Oxford OX2 6DP

Oxford New York

Athens Auckland Bangkok Bogotá Buenos Aires Calcutta Cape Town
Chennai Dar es Salaam Delhi Florence Hong Kong Istanbul Karachi
Kuala Lumpur Madrid Melbourne Mexico City Mumbai Nairobi
Paris São Paulo Singapore Taipei Tokyo Toronto Warsaw
and associated companies in
Berlin Ibadan

OXFORD and OXFORD ENGLISH
are trade marks of Oxford University Press

ISBN 0 19 423049 X

This simplified edition © Oxford University Press 2000

Third impression 2000

First published in Oxford Bookworms 1990
This second edition published in the Oxford Bookworms Library 2000

A complete recording of this Bookworms edition of *Three Men in a Boat*
is available on cassette ISBN 0 19 422741 3

Illustrated by Kate Simpson

Printed in Spain by Unigraf s.l.

CONTENTS

Chapter 1

We decide to go on holiday

There were four of us – George, and William Samuel Harris, and myself, and Montmorency. We were sitting in my room, and we were smoking and talking about how bad we were – ill, I mean, of course.

We were all feeling in poor health, and we were getting quite worried about it. Harris said that he felt really bad sometimes, and he did not know what he was doing. And then George said that he felt bad, too, and that he did not know what he was doing either. With me it was my heart. I knew it was my heart because I had read something in a magazine about the symptoms of a bad heart. I had all of them.

It is a most extraordinary thing, but every time I read about an illness, I realize that I have it too – and that my symptoms are very bad! In fact, my health has always been a worry, I remember . . .

One day I had a little health problem, and I went to the British Museum Library to read about it. I took the book off the library shelf, and I began to read. After some time, I turned over the page and I began to read about another illness. I don't remember the name of the illness, but I know it was something really terrible.

1

I read about half a page – and then I knew that I had that disease too.

I sat there for a time, cold with horror. Slowly, I began to turn over more pages. I came to a disease which was worse than the last one. I began to read about it and, as I expected, I had that disease too. Then I began to get really interested in myself, so I went back to the beginning of the book. I started with the letter 'a' and I read from 'a' to 'z'. I found that there was only one disease which I did not have. This made me a little unhappy. Why didn't I have that disease too?

When I walked into that reading-room, I was a happy, healthy young man. When I left I was a very sick man, close to death . . .

But I was talking about my heart – nobody understood how ill I really was. I had this bad heart when I was a boy. It was with me all the time. I knew that it was my heart because I had all the symptoms of a bad heart. The main symptom was that I did not want to work. Of course, nobody understood that the problem was my heart. Doctors were not so clever then. They just thought that I was lazy!

'Why, you lazy boy, you,' they used to say. 'Get up and do some work for once in your life!' They did not understand that I was ill.

And they did not give me medicine for this illness – they hit me on the side of the head. It is very strange, but those blows on my head often made the illness go away for a time. Sometimes just one blow made the

sickness disappear and made me want to start work
immediately . . .

Anyway, that evening, George and William Harris and I sat
there for half an hour, and described our illnesses to each
other. I explained to George and William Harris how I felt
when I got up in the morning. William Harris told us how
he felt when he went to bed. Then George stood in front of
the fire, and, with great feeling, he showed us how he felt in
the night.

George always thinks he is ill, but really, there is never
anything the matter with him, you know.

At that moment Mrs Poppets, my housekeeper, knocked
on the door. She wanted to know if we were ready to have
supper.

We smiled sadly at each other, and then we said that
perhaps we should try to eat something. Harris said that a
little food helped to prevent illness. So Mrs Poppets brought
the supper in. We sat down at the table, and for half an hour
we managed to play with some steak and chips – and with
a large cake that Mrs Poppets had made.

When we had made ourselves eat something, we filled our
glasses, and we lit our pipes. Then we began to talk about
our health again. We were not quite sure what was the
matter with us. However, we were all quite certain of one
thing – we had been doing too much work.

'We need a rest,' Harris said.

'A rest and a change,' George added.

I agreed with George, and I said that perhaps we could go

Then George, with great feeling, showed us how he felt in the night.

to the country. We could find a nice, quiet place and we could sit in the warm summer sun. We could go somewhere peaceful, far away from other people.

Harris said that he thought that would be awful. He added that he had been to a place like that once. Everyone went to bed at eight o'clock, and he had to walk for an hour to buy cigarettes and a newspaper.

'No,' Harris said. 'If you want a rest and a change, then the sea is best.'

I said that this was a terrible idea. A sea trip is fine if you are going for a month or two – but not for a week. I know what it is like . . .

You start out on Monday and you think that you are going to enjoy yourself. You wave goodbye happily to your friends. You walk up and down on the ship, like Captain Cook, Sir Francis Drake or Christopher Columbus. On Tuesday you wish that you had not come. On Wednesday, Thursday and Friday you wish that you were dead. On Saturday you are able to drink something. You begin to smile a little at the kind people who ask you how you are. On Sunday you start to walk again, and you eat a little. And on Monday morning, as you stand and wait to get off the ship – you begin to enjoy yourself.

I remember that a friend of mine once took a short sea trip from London to Liverpool for his health. He bought a return ticket, but, when he got to Liverpool, he sold it and he came back by train . . .

So I was against the sea trip – not for myself, you understand. I am never seasick. But I was afraid for George. George said he would be fine. In fact, he said he would quite like it, but he thought that Harris and I would both be ill. Harris said he was never seasick. In fact, he had often tried to be ill, but he had not succeeded. It is very strange, but, when you are on land, you never meet anybody who has ever been seasick!

So George said, 'Well, let's go up the river, then.' He added, 'We'll have fresh air on the river. The hard work on the boat will make us hungry, so we'll enjoy our food. We'll sleep well, too.'

Harris replied, 'Well, you never have any trouble sleeping, anyway. In fact, you're always going to sleep!'

But, in the end, Harris agreed that it was a good idea. I thought that it was a good idea, too. The only one who did not like the idea was Montmorency.

'It's different for me,' his face said. 'You like it, but I don't! There's nothing for me to do. I don't smoke. I don't like looking at the trees and the flowers, and when I'm asleep you'll play about with the boat and I'll fall over the side!'

Montmorency's idea of a good time is to collect together all the most awful dogs he can find and then go round the town, looking for other awful dogs to fight.

But we were three to one, so we decided to go anyway.

Chapter 2

We start to make plans

We pulled out the maps and we discussed plans.

We decided to start on the following Saturday. Harris and I would go down to Kingston in the morning and take the boat up to Chertsey, but George could not leave the City until the afternoon. (George goes to sleep at a bank from ten o'clock until four o'clock from Monday to Friday. On Saturday they wake him up and put him out onto the street at two o'clock.) So George was going to meet us at Chertsey.

The next question was where to sleep at night.

George and I did not want to sleep in hotels at night. We wanted to sleep outside. 'How beautiful,' we said, 'in the country, by the river, with the birds, the flowers and the trees all around us!'

I can imagine it easily . . .

At the end of the day, night comes and the world is peaceful and calm. Our little boat moves silently into some quiet little corner on the river. There we put up our tent, and we cook and eat our simple supper. Then we fill our pipes and we sit and talk quietly. Sometimes we stop for a moment or two and we listen to the water as it plays gently against the boat. The silver moon shines down on us and our heads are full of beautiful thoughts. We sit in silence for a time. We do not want to speak. Then we laugh quietly, put away our pipes, say 'Goodnight' and go to bed. The peaceful sound of the water against the boat sends us to sleep – and we dream. We dream that the world is young again . . .

'And what about when it rains?' Harris said.

He was right. When it rains, you do not enjoy living in tents.

I thought about it again . . .

It is evening. You are very wet. There is a lot of water in the boat and everything in it is wet, too. You find a place on the river bank which is not as wet as other places. You get out of the boat, pull out the tent, and two of you try to put it up. Because it is wet, it is very heavy. And then it falls on top of you. You cannot get it off your head, and you get angry. All the time it is raining heavily. It is difficult to put up a tent in good weather. In wet weather it is almost impossible. The other man does not help you. He starts to play about. You get your side of the tent up and begin to tie the ropes to the ground. Just then he pulls the tent from his side, and he destroys all your hard work.

'Here! What do you think you're doing?' you call out.

'What are you doing, you mean,' he answers angrily.

'Don't pull it! You've got it all wrong, you stupid man!' you cry.

'No, I haven't!' he shouts. 'Let your side go!'

'I tell you, you're wrong!' you scream, and you wish

It is almost impossible to put up a tent in wet weather.

you could get to him to hit him. You pull your side of the tent hard – and pull out all the ropes on *his* side.

'Ah! The stupid fool!' you hear him say to himself. And then, suddenly, he gives a violent pull – and your side comes out, too. Slowly, you start to go round to his side to tell him what you think of him. At the same time, he begins to come round the other way, to tell you what he feels. And you follow each other round and round, and you shout at each other – until the tent falls down. And there you are! You stand and look at each other across the tent. At the same time, you both call out, 'There you are! What did I tell you?'

Meanwhile, the third man has been trying to get the water out of the boat. The water has run up his arms, and he is wet and angry. Suddenly, he wants to know what you are doing, and why the tent is not up yet.

When, at last, the tent is up, you carry the things out of the boat. Supper is mostly rainwater – rainwater bread, rainwater soup. Happily, you have something strong to drink. This brings back your interest in life until it is time to go to bed.

There you dream that a very large animal has suddenly sat down on you. You wake up and you understand that something terrible has happened. At first, you think that the world has ended. Then you think that this cannot be true. So it must be thieves, or murderers, or fire. No help comes, and all you know is that thousands of people are kicking you, and you cannot breathe.

Somebody else is in trouble, too. You can hear his cries. They are coming from under your bed.

You decide to fight, and you hit out, left and right, with your arms and your legs. You are shouting all the time. At last you find your head in the fresh air. Near you, you see a half-dressed murderer. He is waiting to kill you. You are just going to start fighting him when you see that it is Jim.

At the same moment, he sees that it is you.

'Oh, it's you, is it?' he says.

'Yes,' you answer. 'What's happened?'

'The tent has blown down, I think,' he says. 'Where's Bill?'

Then you both shout for Bill. The ground underneath you moves, and a voice says, 'Get off my head!'

The next day you have no voices because you have all caught colds, and all day you argue with each other in angry whispers . . .

We therefore decided that we would sleep out in tents on fine nights, and in hotels when it rained.

Montmorency was very pleased about this. He does not like peace and quiet. He prefers noise. But he looks so good, so well-behaved. When old ladies and gentlemen look at him, tears come into their eyes.

When he first came to live with me, I thought, 'This dog will not be with me long. He is too good for this world.' But, by the end of the year, he had killed twelve chickens, which I had to pay for . . . I had pulled him out of a hundred and fourteen street fights . . . A woman had brought me a dead cat and had called me a murderer. Then I changed my ideas about Montmorency.

We had decided where to sleep, so now we had to discuss what to take with us. We began to argue about this, so we agreed that we had done enough for one night.

Chapter 3

We decide what to take

The following evening, we discussed what we wanted to take with us. Harris said, 'Now get me a piece of paper, J., and write everything down. George, you get a pencil, and I'll make the list.'

That's Harris – he tells everybody what to do, and they do all the work. I remember that my Uncle Podger was like Harris . . .

Everybody in the house had to help when Uncle Podger did a job. When they bought a picture once, Aunt Podger asked, 'Now, where shall we put this?'

'Oh, I'll do it. Don't worry about it. I'll do it all myself,' he said. And then he took off his coat to begin. He sent one of the girls out to buy some nails, and then he sent one of the boys to tell her how big

12

the nails ought to be. 'Now, Bill, you go and get my hammer,' he shouted. 'And bring me a ruler, Tom. And Jim, I need a ladder – and a kitchen chair, too. Maria, you stay here to hold the light – and Tom, come here! You can give me the picture.'

Then he lifted the picture up . . . and he dropped it. He tried to catch the glass . . . and he cut himself. He looked for something to put round his finger, and he could not find anything. So he danced round the house, and he shouted at everybody.

Half an hour later, the finger had been tied up, they had bought new glass, and everything was ready. Uncle Podger tried again. Everybody stood round him. They were all ready to help. Two people held the chair, a third helped him to get on it, a fourth gave him a nail, and a fifth passed him the hammer. He took the nail . . . and he dropped it!

'There,' he said sadly. 'Now the nail's gone.'

So everybody got down on the ground to look for it. At last we found the nail, but then he lost the hammer.

'Where's the hammer? What did I do with the hammer? There are seven of you there, and you don't know where the hammer is!'

We found the hammer for him, but then he lost the place on the wall where he was going to put the picture. So each one of us had to get up on the chair and look for the place. And each one of us thought that it was a different place. Then Uncle Podger tried again himself. This time he fell off the chair on to the piano. His head and his body hit the piano at the same

13

time. The music was beautiful, but Uncle Podger's words were not! Aunt Maria was not pleased. She said that she did not want the children to listen to those terrible words. She added calmly, 'The next time that you are going to put a picture on the wall, please tell me. Then I can arrange to go and spend a week with my mother.'

Uncle Podger got up and tried again, and at midnight the picture was on the wall. It was not very straight, and everyone was very tired and unhappy. Uncle Podger looked at the picture proudly and said, 'You see, it was only a little job!' . . .

Harris is like that. So I told him that George would write down the list, and I would do the work. He could get the pencil and the paper.

The first list was too long. So we started again.

'Now,' George said, 'we don't want to take a tent. We can put a cover over the boat at night. It will be like a little house, lovely and warm and comfortable. It's much easier than a tent.'

Then we made a list of all the clothes we needed. George told us that he knew all about this kind of thing – and we believed him. We discovered later that this was not true.

Next we talked about the food.

'First, breakfast,' George began. 'We need eggs, cold meat, tea, bread and butter, of course. And for dinner we can take cold chicken legs, tomatoes, cold meat, fruit, cakes, chocolate . . . We can drink water.' Then he added, 'And we can take a bottle of whisky, too – for when we are sick, you know.'

We did not wish to talk about being sick. But later, we were glad we had taken the whisky.

So we made our list, and it was a long one.

Chapter 4

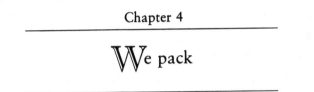

We pack

The next day, which was Friday, we collected all these things together. In the evening we met to pack.

We got a big suitcase for the clothes. There were two large baskets with lids, for the food and for the pans and things to cook with. We moved the table over to the window. Then we put everything in the middle of the floor.

After we had done that, we sat there and we looked at it.

I said that I would pack.

I think that I am very good at packing. It is one of the things that I do best. So I told the others that I would organize it. They agreed to this idea too quickly. That was rather strange. George lit his pipe and sat back in the armchair. Harris put his feet on the table and lit a cigarette.

This was not, of course, what I had expected. When I said that I would organize it, I meant that I would tell them what to do. Then I would sit and watch them do it.

However, I said nothing, and I started to pack the clothes. It took much longer than I had expected, but in the end it was finished. I sat on the suitcase and closed it. George and Harris watched me with great interest.

'Aren't you going to put the boots in?' Harris asked.

I looked round, and saw the boots. Why did Harris wait until I had closed the suitcase?

George laughed quietly.

I opened the suitcase, and I put the boots in. It was not easy! And just as I was going to close the suitcase again, an awful idea came to me. Had I packed my toothbrush?

Of course, I had to look for it, and, of course, I could not find it. I had to take everything out again. I found George's toothbrush. I found Harris's toothbrush, but I could not find mine. In the end, I found it inside a boot.

I packed everything again.

When I had finished, George asked if the soap was in the suitcase. I said I did not care about the soap. I threw down the lid of the suitcase, and I closed it again. Then I found my cigarettes were inside it.

I finished the suitcase at five past ten, and the food was still not packed!

Harris said, 'We have to start the holiday in twelve hours. Perhaps George and I had better do the rest of the packing.'

I agreed, and I sat down.

They began quite happily. I said nothing. I only waited. I looked at all the plates and cups, and bottles, and tomatoes, and cakes, etc. I felt that it was soon going to get exciting.

It did. They started by breaking a cup. That was just to show you what they could do and to get you interested. Then Harris packed a pan on top of a tomato and . . . well, they had to pick out the tomato with a teaspoon.

And then it was George's turn, and he stepped on the butter. I did not say anything, but I got up and went over to the table and watched them. This annoyed them more than anything, and it made them worried and excited. They stepped on things, and they put things behind them. And then they could not find them when they wanted them. They packed soft things at the bottom of the basket, and then put heavy things on top of them.

Then it got worse. After George got the butter off his shoe, they tried to put it in the teapot. At first they could not get it in. Then, when they did get it in, they decided that the teapot was the wrong place. But they could not get the butter out again. However, in the end they did manage to get it out and they put it down on a chair. Harris sat on it, and when he stood up, the butter stuck to his trousers. Then they looked for the butter all over the room. In the end, George got behind Harris, and he saw it.

'There it is!' he cried.

'Where?' Harris asked, and he turned round quickly.

'Stand still!' George shouted.

When they got the butter off Harris, they packed it in the teapot again.

Montmorency was in all this, of course. He sat down on

Montmorency pretended that the oranges were rats, and he got into the food basket and killed three of them.

things just when George and Harris were going to pack them; he put his leg into the sugar; he ran away with the teaspoons. He pretended that the oranges were rats, and he got into the food basket and killed three of them.

The packing was completed at ten to one in the morning, and we all went to bed. George said, 'What time shall I wake you two?'

Harris said, 'Seven.'

I said 'Six.'

In the end we said, 'Wake us at half past six, George.'

Chapter 5

We start our holiday

It was Mrs Poppets who woke me the next morning. She said, 'Do you know that it's nearly nine o'clock, sir?'

'What!' I cried, and I jumped out of bed. I woke Harris and told him.

He said, 'I thought you told us to get up at six?'

'I did,' I answered.

'Well, why didn't you wake me then?' he asked. 'Now we won't be on the water until after twelve o'clock.'

Then we remembered. We looked at George. He was still asleep. Now, it makes me very angry when I see another man

19

asleep and I am awake. We decided to wake George. We ran across the room, and we pulled the bedclothes off him. Harris hit him with a shoe, and I shouted in his ear. He woke up.

'Wh. . .aa. . .t,' he began.

'Get up, you fat, lazy thing!' Harris shouted. 'It's a quarter to ten!'

Then we began to get ready, and we remembered that we had packed the toothbrushes. So we had to go downstairs to get them out of the suitcase.

Finally, we were ready and Harris said, 'We need a good breakfast inside us today.' While we were eating, George got the newspaper and read us interesting pieces from it – pieces about people who had been killed on the river, and interesting reports about the weather. The weather report for that day said, 'Rain, cold, wet to fine, some thunder, and an east wind'. But weather reports make me angry anyway. They always tell you what the weather was like yesterday, or the day before. It is never today's weather. It is always wrong. I remember that one autumn I went on holiday . . .

On that holiday, the weather reports in the newspaper were always wrong. On Monday it said, 'Heavy rain, with thunder'. So we did not go out that day. All day people passed our house. They were all going out, happy and smiling. The sun was shining and there were no clouds in the sky.

'Ah,' we said, as we watched them, 'they'll be very wet when they come back, though.'

And we laughed. Then we sat down by the fire and read our books.

At twelve o'clock the room was too hot, and the sun was still shining.

'Well, it will rain this afternoon, then,' we told ourselves.

The rain never came.

The next morning, we read that it was going to be sunny and very hot. So we dressed in light clothes, and we went out. Half an hour later, it began to rain hard, and a very cold wind blew up. And this went on all day. We came home with colds, and we went to bed . . .

But on the morning of our holiday it was bright and sunny, and George could not make us unhappy. So he went to work.

Harris and I finished the rest of the breakfast. Then we carried all our luggage into the road. We tried to get a taxi. Usually taxis come along every three minutes. In fact, there are usually too many taxis. However, that morning we waited twenty minutes for a taxi. A crowd of interested people collected to watch us. I think it was because we had so much luggage. There was a big suitcase, a small bag, two baskets, several blankets, some fruit in a brown paper bag, some pans, some umbrellas and four or five coats and raincoats. After a very long time, a taxi arrived and stopped for us. We packed our things into it, kicked two of Montmorency's friends out of the taxi, and started on our holiday. The crowd of people waved goodbye to us.

Chapter 6

On the river

At Kingston our boat was waiting for us. Harris and I put all our things into it, and we moved off along the River Thames. Montmorency was at the front of the boat. We travelled along the river without any accidents. Well, there was only one little accident. That was when the boat hit the river bank, and Harris fell over backwards. When we came to Hampton Court Palace, Harris asked me if I had ever been in the maze there. He told me a story about it . . .

He went into the maze once, to show a friend the way. He had studied a map of the maze, and so he knew it was very easy to get out of it again. Harris said to his friend, 'We'll just go in and walk around for ten minutes, and then we'll come out and get some lunch. It's easy, you see. You just keep taking the first turning to the right.'

Soon after they had gone in, they met some people. These people said that they had been there for three quarters of an hour. They said they wanted to get out. Harris said, 'Follow me! I'm going out myself in about ten minutes.'

The people all said that Harris was very kind, and they began to follow him.

Harris in the maze at Hampton Court Palace.

As they were going along, they collected other people who wanted to get out. In the end, all the people in the maze were following Harris. There were about twenty of them. Some of them had thought that they were never going to see their friends and their families again. One woman was carrying a baby. She held on to Harris's arm because she did not want to lose him.

Harris continued to turn to the right, but it seemed to be a long way. At last, Harris's friend said to him, 'This must be a very big maze.'

'One of the biggest in Europe,' Harris answered.

'Yes, it must be,' his friend continued, 'because we've walked about three kilometres already.'

Harris began to think that it was rather strange, but he went on. After some time, they came to a piece of cake on the ground. Harris's friend said that they had passed the piece of cake earlier. Harris replied, 'No! Impossible!'

The woman with the baby said, 'No, I took it from the baby, and I threw it there myself. It was just before we met you. In fact, I wish I never had met you,' she added.

Harris got angry then, and he took out his map. He showed it to the people, but one man said, 'A map's no good when you don't know where you are.'

So then Harris said that the best thing was to go back to the entrance and start again. Everybody agreed, and they all turned and followed Harris the other way.

After ten minutes they found themselves in the centre of the maze. Harris was going to pretend that he wanted to be in the centre, but the crowd looked dangerous. So Harris decided to say that it was an accident.

Anyway, now they knew where they were on the map, and it looked easy. So they all started off again for the third time.

And three minutes later, they were back in the centre again.

After that, every time they tried again, they arrived back in the centre. Harris took out his map again, but this made the crowd angry. They told him what to do with his map. Harris felt that the crowd was not very grateful to him.

Then they all started to shout, and in the end the keeper came. He climbed up a ladder, and he called to them, 'Wait, there! I'll come and get you.'

But he was a young keeper, and he was new to the job, so when he got into the maze, he could not find them. Then he got lost. From time to time, they saw him as he ran past, on the other side of the hedge. He shouted, 'Wait there! I'm coming!'

Then, five minutes later, he appeared again in the same place. He asked them why they had moved.

They had to wait for one of the old keepers to come back from lunch and let them out . . .

Harris said that it was a fine maze, and we agreed that we would try to get George into it on the way back.

The River Thames from Kingston to Oxford.

Chapter 7

Harris gets angry

Harris told me about the maze as we were passing through Molesey lock. Our boat was the only one in the lock that day. Usually it is very busy. On Sundays, when the weather is fine, there are boats everywhere. Everybody comes down to the river. They wear brightly coloured clothes, and the river is full of colour – yellow, and blue, and orange, and green, and white, and red and pink.

At Hampton Harris wanted to get out and have a look at the church there, but I refused to stop. I have never liked visiting churches, but Harris loves them. He said, 'I've looked forward to visiting Hampton Church ever since we decided to make this trip.' He added, 'I only came on the trip because I thought we were going there!'

I reminded him about George. I said, 'We've got to get the boat up to Shepperton by five o'clock to meet him.'

Then Harris got angry with George. 'Why does George have to play around all day? Why has he left us with this big, heavy boat to tow up and down the river? Why couldn't George come and do some work? Why didn't he take a day's holiday and come down with us? The bank! Ha! What good is he at the bank?' He stopped for a moment and then he continued, 'I never see him doing any work there. He sits behind a bit of glass all day, and he pretends to do something. What's the good of a man behind a bit of glass? I have to work. Why can't George work? What does he do at the bank? What good are banks, anyway? They take all your money, and then, when you write out a cheque, they send it back! They say you've spent all your money! What's the good of that? If George was here, we could go to see that church. Anyway, I don't believe he's at the bank. He's playing about somewhere, that's what he's doing. And we've got to do all the work! . . . I'm going to get out and have a drink!'

I told him that there were no pubs nearby, and then he started shouting about the river. 'What good is the river? We'll all die of thirst! No pubs!' (It's better to let Harris go on shouting when he gets angry. Then he gets tired, and he is quiet afterwards.)

I reminded him that we had water in the boat. Then he started shouting about water. He said drinks like that made people ill.

However, he said that he must drink something. He climbed onto the seat and he bent down to get the bottle out of the basket. It was at the bottom, and he had to bend down, lower and lower. At the same time, he was trying to steer the boat, and he pulled the wrong rope. The boat turned sharply and bumped into the bank of the river, and Harris fell into the basket. He stood there on his head, and he held on to the side of the boat. His legs were in the air. He could not move in case he fell over. He had to stay there until I could catch his legs and pull him back. And that made him more angry.

We stopped under the trees by Kempton Park, and we had lunch. It is very pretty there, on the grass by the river, under the trees. We had an excellent meal, and Harris calmed down and began to enjoy himself again.

By half past three, we had reached Sunbury lock. Then we went up to Walton, which is quite an interesting place. Julius Caesar stayed there with his soldiers. Queen Elizabeth I, she was there too. You can never get away from that woman. She was everywhere.

Next we came to Halliford and Shepperton. There is an old church at Shepperton, and I was worried in case Harris wanted to go and visit it. I saw him looking towards it as we came near, but I moved the boat quickly, and Harris's cap fell into the water. We had to get it back, of course. Luckily, he was very angry with me, and so he forgot about his church.

As we came up to the lock at Weybridge, we saw something brightly coloured on one of the lock gates. When we looked closer, we saw that it was George. Montmorency started to bark madly. I shouted, and Harris called out wildly. George waved his cap and yelled back to us. The lock-keeper ran out because he thought someone had fallen in the water. He seemed annoyed when he saw that no one had fallen in.

Chapter 8

George starts work

We decided that now George was there, he was going to do some work. He did not want to work, of course. 'I've had a bad day at the bank,' he explained.

Harris, who is sometimes a little cruel, said, 'Ah! And now you're going to have a bad time on the river for a change. A change is good for you. Come on! Get out of the boat and tow!'

George could not refuse, really, but he did say, 'Perhaps it would be better if I stayed in the boat and prepared the meal. You two can tow the boat.' Then he added, 'It's very difficult to prepare a meal and you both look tired.'

Our only reply was to give him the rope. So he started walking, and he pulled the boat behind him.

Sometimes people forget that they are towing a boat, and later, George told us a story about this . . .

George had once seen a man and a young lady who were walking by the side of the river. They were pulling a rope behind them and they were talking to each other. They did not notice that there was no boat on the end of the rope. Of course, they probably had a boat on the end of the rope when they started out. But it had disappeared. The two young people were

not worried about this. They had their rope. They did
not seem to care that there was no boat. George was
going to call out to tell them about it. But, just then,
he had an idea. He took hold of the rope, and he tied
it to his own boat. Then he and his three fat, heavy
friends sat in the back of their boat, and lit their pipes.
And that young man and young woman towed George
and his friends up to Marlow. It was when they
reached the lock that they looked back. Suddenly they
understood that they had been towing the wrong
boat. George said, 'I've never seen anyone look as sad
as those two young people then!'

The young man was a bit annoyed. In fact, he was
probably going to say something angry to George and
his friends. But just then, the young woman cried
wildly, 'Oh, Henry, then where's Aunt Mary?' . . .

'Did they ever get the old lady back?' Harris asked. George
replied that he did not know.

But the most exciting thing of all is to let girls tow your
boat. Let me tell you about it . . .

First of all, you need three girls. You always need three
girls to tow a boat. Two of them hold the rope, and the
other one runs here and there and laughs all the time.

They usually begin by tying themselves up in the
rope. They get it round their legs, and then they have
to sit down to untie it. Next, they get it round their
necks. When they finally get it right, they always start
by running. They pull the boat much too fast. After a
few minutes, they are tired, and so they stop suddenly.

The most exciting thing of all is to let girls tow your boat.

They all sit down on the grass, and they start to laugh. Meanwhile, your boat goes out into the middle of the river, and it starts to turn round. Then they stand up and are surprised.

'Oh, look!' they say. 'The boat's gone into the middle of the river!'

After this, they pull you along quite well for a time. Then one of them decides to stop for something else. So the boat runs aground in shallow water near the river bank. You jump up, and you push the boat off into deep water. You shout to them, 'Don't stop!'

'Yes, what's the matter?' they shout back.

'Don't stop!' you cry loudly.

'Don't what?'

'Don't stop . . . go on . . . go on!'

'Go back, Emily, and see what they want,' one of them says.

And Emily comes back and asks, 'What is it? Is anything wrong?'

'No!' you shout. 'It's all right! But go on! Don't stop!'

'Why not?'

'Because we can't steer the boat if you stop.'

'Why not?'

'You must keep the boat moving!'

'Oh, all right. I'll tell them. Are we doing everything else all right?'

'Oh, yes, very nicely – but don't stop!'

'I see. Oh, give me my hat, please. It's over there.'

You find her hat, and you give it to her. But then

another girl comes. She thinks she will have her hat, too. And then they take Mary's hat for her. Mary does not want it, so they bring it back. Then they want a comb.It is about twenty minutes before they start again. Then, at the next corner, they see a cow. You have to stop, and leave the boat, to chase the cow away . . .

Anyway, this time it was George who towed us on to Penton Hook. There we discussed the important question of where to spend the night. We had decided to sleep on the boat. Therefore we could stay there, or we could go on past Staines. In the end, we decided to continue to Runnymede.

Later we all wished we had stopped at Penton Hook.

Chapter 9

Our first night on the boat

After some time, Harris and I began to think that Bell Weir lock had disappeared. 'Perhaps someone has taken it away,' we said. George had towed the boat as far as Staines, and we had towed it from there. It seemed to get heavier and heavier. We began to think that we were right and that someone had moved the lock. But, finally, at half past seven, we reached it and got through it. By now we just wanted to eat and to go to bed. So we stopped before we reached

Magna Charta Island. It was quite a pretty place and we tied our boat to a big tree.

We were looking forward to having something to eat then, but George said, 'No! It's better to put the cover on the boat first, before it gets too dark. All our work will be finished then. We'll be able to sit down and enjoy our meal.'

None of us had realized that it would be so difficult to fix the cover. There were five pieces of metal and you put these into special holes on the side of the boat. The pieces of metal were half circles, and when you had put them into the holes, you just had to pull the cover over them.

We thought it would probably take about ten minutes.

We were wrong.

We took the pieces of metal, and we began to drop them into their holes. You would not expect this to be dangerous work, but it was.

First of all, the pieces of metal would not fit into their holes. We had to jump on them, and kick them, and beat them. And when we got one in, we found that it was the wrong piece of metal for those holes. So we had to take it out again.

At last we got them finished. Then we only had to put the cover on. George took one end, and he fastened it over the front of the boat. Harris stood in the middle of the boat to take the cover from George. I stayed at the back of the boat to take the end of the cover from Harris.

George did his job all right, but it was new work to Harris and he did everything wrong.

I do not know how he did it, and Harris himself could not explain it later. After ten minutes of really hard work, he was inside the cover. He could not get out. He fought the cover hard – and knocked George over. Then George got angry and he began to fight, too. George could not get out of the cover either.

At the time, I did not know anything about all this. I did not understand what was happening anyway. They had told Montmorency and me to stand and wait. So Montmorency and I stood there and waited. We could see that the cover was moving about quite violently. However, we thought that it was all necessary for the job. We did nothing because they had told us to wait.

We also heard many bad words coming from under the cover. Montmorency and I decided that this was because the job was very difficult.

We waited for some time, but everything seemed to get worse. Finally George's head appeared over the side of the boat. It said,

'We can't breathe under here! Why don't you help us, you great stupid thing!'

So I went and helped them. Harris's face was nearly black, so I was just in time.

It took another half an hour after that to fix the cover. And then we started to prepare supper. We needed some hot water to make tea, so we put the water on the stove at the front of the boat, and we went to the back. We pretended that we were not interested in the water at all. We wanted

'*Why don't you help us, you great stupid thing!*' *cried George.*

it to think we did not care if it got hot or not. We began to get the other things out.

That is the only way to get hot water on the river. If the water knows that you are waiting for it, it will never get hot. You have to go away and begin your meal without it. You must not look at it. Then you will soon hear it making a lot of noise, because it wants to be made into tea.

It is also a good idea to talk very loudly to each other. You must say that you do not want any tea, that you do not need any tea, and that you are not going to have any tea. You get very near the water and you shout,

'I don't want any tea. Do you, George?'

And George shouts back, 'Oh, no. I don't like tea. We'll have milk.'

This makes the water very angry, and it gets hot very fast.

We did this, and, when everything else was ready, the tea was ready, too. Then we sat down to have supper. We really wanted that supper. We needed that supper. And for thirty-five minutes nobody on the boat spoke.

After supper, we sat and smiled at each other. We smiled at Montmorency, too. We loved everybody. We sat back, we lit our pipes, and we began to talk.

George told us about something very funny that happened to his father once . . .

When he was young, George's father was travelling with a friend. One night they stopped at a little hotel. They spent the evening there with some other young men. After a very happy evening they went to bed. It was late, and, by that time, they (George's father and George's father's friend) were feeling quite happy themselves. Anyway, they were going to sleep in the same room, but in different beds. When they got into the room, they dropped their light, which went out. So they had to undress and get into bed in the dark. They thought they were getting into separate beds. However, because they could not see, they both got into the same one. One of them got in with his head at the top of the bed. The other one got in on the other side of the bed. He lay with his feet by the first one's head.

Nobody spoke for a moment. Then George's father said, 'Joe!'

'What's the matter, Tom?' Joe replied, from the other end of the bed.

'Why, there's a man in my bed,' George's father said. 'His feet are here, next to me.'

'Well, that's very strange, Tom,' Joe answered, 'but there's a man in my bed, too.'

'What are you going to do?' George's father asked.

'Well, I'm going to throw him out,' Joe replied.

'So am I,' George's father said, bravely.

There was a short fight, and then there were two heavy bangs on the floor. After a moment or two, a rather sad voice said, 'I say, Tom!'

'Yes?'

'How have you got on?'

'Well, to tell the truth, my man's thrown me out.'

'My man's thrown me out, too . . . I say, this isn't a very good hotel, is it?' . . .

At the end of George's story, Harris asked, 'What was the name of the hotel?'

'The Riverside,' George replied. 'Why?'

'Ah, it isn't the same hotel, then,' Harris answered.

'What do you mean?' George asked.

'Well, it's strange,' Harris said, 'but the same thing happened to my father once. I've often heard him tell the story.'

After that, we went to bed, but I slept very badly.

Chapter 10

Our first morning

I woke up at six o'clock the next morning, and I found that George was awake, too. We both tried to go to sleep again, but we could not. This was because we did not need to get up early. We could sleep for another two or three hours. But we both felt we would die if we tried to sleep for another five minutes.

George said that the same thing had happened to him a few months before. He told me a story about it . . .

At that time George had rooms in the house of a lady called Mrs Gippings. One evening his watch stopped at a quarter past eight. He did not realize this then.

When he went to bed, he took off his watch, and he did not look at it.

This happened in the winter, so it was dark in the mornings, anyway. When George woke up, he looked at his watch. It was a quarter past eight.

'Good heavens!' George cried. 'I have to be at the bank by nine o'clock!' And he threw down the watch and jumped out of bed. He had a cold bath and he dressed. Then he ran and looked at his watch. It had started to go again, and it was twenty to nine.

George took his watch and ran downstairs. The dining-room was dark and silent. There was no fire, no breakfast. George was very angry with Mrs G. He decided to tell her this later, in the evening. Then he caught hold of his coat, his hat and his umbrella, and ran to the front door. It was locked! George said that Mrs G. was a lazy old woman. Then he unlocked the door and ran out into the street.

For a few hundred metres he ran as fast as he could. But, suddenly, he noticed that there were not many people about. He also noticed that the shops were not open. It was a very dark and foggy morning. However, it seemed very strange that they had closed the shops because of the fog. He had to go to work, so why should other people stay in bed?

George could see only three people. One of them was a policeman, one was a man who was taking vegetables to the market, and one was a taxi-driver.

George looked at his watch. It was five to nine. For a moment, he stood there without moving. He wondered if he was dreaming. He felt his wrist, and bent down and felt his legs. Then, with his watch in his hand, he went up to the policeman.

'What time is it, please?' he asked the policeman.

'What's the time?' the policeman repeated. 'Well, listen.'

Just then George heard a clock . . . one . . . two . . . three. 'But that's only three times!' George said, when it had finished.

'Well, how many times do you want?' the policeman replied.

'Why, nine, of course,' George said, and he held out his watch to the policeman.

'Do you know where you live?' the policeman asked.

George thought for a minute, and then he told the policeman the address.

'Well, I think you should go back there quietly,' the policeman continued. 'And take your watch with you!'

So George went back.

At first, he thought he would go to bed again. However, he did not like the idea of having to get up again later. So he decided to go to sleep in the armchair.

But he could not get to sleep. He tried to read, but that was no good either. Finally, he put on his coat again, and he went out for a walk.

He felt very lonely and miserable. He met policemen who looked at him strangely. They followed him about. He began to feel that he really had done something wrong. He started to hide in dark corners whenever he saw a policeman.

Of course, then the policemen wanted to know what he was doing. George said, 'Nothing. I'm just going for a walk.' But they did not believe him. In the end, two policemen went back to the house with him. They wanted to know if he really did live there. They watched him go in with his key. Then they stood on the opposite side of the road, and they watched the house.

When he got in, he thought, 'I'll light the fire, and then I'll make some breakfast.' But he made a lot of noise, and he was afraid that Mrs Gippings would wake up. She would hear the noise and think that he was a burglar. Then she would open the window and shout, 'Help! Police!' The two policemen would come and arrest George, and take him away. So he stopped trying to prepare breakfast, and he put on his coat. Then he sat in the armchair and he waited for Mrs Gippings. She came down at half past seven.

George said that, since then, he had never got up too early again . . .

When George had finished his story, we decided to wake up Harris. It was hard work. In the end we had to use quite a sharp piece of metal. Harris sat up suddenly then. Montmorency had been asleep on Harris's chest, and he went flying across the boat.

After that, we pulled up the cover and we put our heads over the side of the boat. We looked down at the water. The night before, we had decided to get up early. We would throw off the cover and we would jump into the water, with shouts of happiness. Then we would enjoy a long swim.

But now that morning had come, it did not seem to be a very good idea. The water looked wet and cold. The wind felt cold, too.

'Well, who's going to go in for a swim first?' Harris said finally.

Nobody hurried to be the first one. George put his head back inside the boat. Montmorency barked with horror at the idea. Harris said it would be difficult to climb back into the boat again from the water. Then he went back into the boat to look for his trousers.

I did not want to give up the idea absolutely. I decided to go down to the edge of the river, and then splash some water over myself. So I went out on to the river bank, and I began to move carefully along the branch of a tree which was over the water.

It was very cold, and I thought I would not splash water over myself, after all. I would go back into the boat and dress. I turned – and just then the stupid branch broke. The next minute, I was in the middle of the river, with half a litre of the Thames inside me.

'Good heavens! Old J.'s gone in!' Harris said.

'Is it all right?' George called out.

'Lovely,' I replied. 'Why don't you come in?'

But they did not want to.

When I got back to the boat, I was very cold. I wanted to put on my shirt as quickly as possible. By accident, I dropped it into the water. This made me very angry, but George started to laugh. 'I can't see anything to laugh at,' I told George. He just went on laughing! In fact, I never saw a man

It seemed to be very difficult work. Whenever he went near the pan, he burnt himself. Then he dropped everything, and danced about, and waved his hands, and shouted. In fact, every time George and I looked at him, he was doing this. At first we thought it was necessary to do this to cook the eggs.

Once Montmorency went and looked into the pan, but he burnt himself. Then he started dancing and shouting, too. It was all very exciting, and George and I were quite sorry when it finished.

Chapter 11

Hotels and tinned fruit

After breakfast I was sitting by the river, and thinking, when George said, 'Perhaps, when you've rested enough, you could help to wash the plates and things.' So I cleaned the pan with some wood and grass – and George's wet shirt.

Then we started to move up the river again, past Old Windsor, which is very pretty. After that, the river is not very interesting until you get to Boveney. George and I were towing the boat then. As we were passing Datchet, George asked me if I remembered our first trip up the river. On that trip we reached Datchet at ten o'clock at night. All we wanted to do was to eat and go to bed.

I replied, 'Yes, I do remember it.' I remember it well. In fact, it will be some time before I forget it . . .

It was one Saturday in August. There was George, and Harris, and me. We were tired and hungry. When we got to Datchet, we took out of the boat the basket of food, the two bags, and the coats and things. Then we began to look for somewhere to stay. We passed a very pretty little hotel, but there were no roses round the door. I wanted somewhere with roses round the door. I do not know why. Anyway, I said, 'Oh, we don't want to go there. Let's look for a little hotel with roses round the door.'

So we went on until we came to another hotel. That was a very nice one, too, and it did have roses. But Harris did not like the man who was standing by the front door. Harris said that he did not look like a nice man, and he was wearing ugly boots. So we went on. We walked for some time, but we did not see any more hotels. Then we met a man and we decided to ask him.

'Excuse me, do you know any nice little hotels near here?' we said.

'Well,' he said, 'you're coming away from them. Go back, and you'll come to the Black Horse.'

We said, 'Oh, we've been there, and we didn't like it. There were no roses round the door.'

'Well, then,' he said, 'there's the Travellers' Rest just beyond it. Have you tried that?'

Harris replied that we did not want to go there. We did not like the man who was staying there. Harris did not like the colour of his hair. He did not like his boots either.

'Well, I don't know what you're going to do, then,' the man answered, 'because they are the only two hotels here.'

'No other hotels!' Harris cried.

'None,' the man replied.

'What are we going to do now?' Harris asked.

Then George spoke. He said, 'You two can ask someone to build you a hotel. I'm going back to the Black Horse!'

So we went back to the Black Horse.

'Good evening,' the man at the desk said.

'Oh, good evening,' George answered. 'We want three beds, please.'

'I'm sorry, sir,' the man replied, 'but we haven't got three beds.'

'Oh, well, it doesn't matter – two beds, then. Two of us can sleep in one bed, can't we?' George continued. He looked at Harris and me.

Harris said, 'Oh, yes.' He thought that George and I could sleep in one bed very easily.

'I'm very sorry, sir,' the man repeated. 'We haven't got any beds. We've already got three men in one bed.'

We picked up our things, and we went over to the Travellers' Rest. It was a pretty little place. I said I thought it was better than the other hotel. Harris said it would be all right. We would not look at the man with red hair and ugly boots.

The people at the Travellers' Rest did not wait to hear what we wanted. The lady at the desk said she had already sent away fourteen people. There was no room of any kind. We asked her if she knew somewhere we could spend the night. She said there was a little house along the road . . .

We did not wait. We picked up the basket, the bags and the coats, and we ran along the road.

The people there laughed at us. There were only three beds in the house, and there were seven men there already.

Someone said, 'Why don't you try the little shop next to the Black Horse?'

So we went back along the road, but there were no beds at the little shop. However, there was an old lady in the shop. She said she had a friend who had some rooms. She added that she would take us there.

The old woman walked very slowly, and it took us twenty minutes to get to her friend's house. During the walk, she told us about all the pains she had in her back. When we got there, there were already some people in her friend's rooms. From there we went to number 27. Number 27 was full. They sent us to number 32, and number 32 was full.

Then we went back along the road. Suddenly Harris sat down on the basket. He said he was not going to move. He added that it seemed to be nice and quiet there, and he said that he would like to die there.

Just then, a little boy came past. 'Do you know any old people that we can frighten, so that they will give us their beds?' we asked him.

'No, I don't,' the boy answered, but he added that

his mother would give us a room. And that was where
we spent the night – in two very short beds.

After that, we were never quite so difficult about
hotels . . .

On our present trip, though, nothing exciting happened. We
continued slowly on our way, and we stopped for lunch near
Monkey Island.

We decided to have cold meat for lunch. Then, after that,
George brought out a tin of fruit. We love tinned fruit, all
three of us. We looked at the picture on the tin. We thought
about the fruit. We imagined the taste of it. We smiled at
each other, and Harris got out a spoon. Then we looked for
the tin-opener. We took everything out of the big basket. We
took everything out of the bags. There was no tin-opener.
We pulled up the boards at the bottom of the boat. We put
everything out on the grass by the river, and we shook
everything. There was no tin-opener!

Then Harris tried to open the tin with a little knife, and
he cut himself badly. George tried with some scissors. The
scissors flew up, and nearly hit him in the eye. I tried to make
a hole in the tin with the sharp end of a piece of metal. But
I missed. As a result, I fell in the water, and the tin flew away
and broke a cup.

Then we all got angry. We took that tin, and we put it on
the grass by the river. Harris went into a field and got a big,
sharp stone. I got a long, thick piece of wood. George held
the tin, and Harris put the sharp end of his stone against the
top of it. I took the piece of wood, and held it high in the

air. Then I brought it down as hard as I could.

It was George's hat that saved his life that day. He keeps that hat now. On a winter evening, when men are telling stories about the dangers they have known, George brings out his hat. He shows it to his friends. Then he tells the story again – and he adds more details to it each time.

Harris was not hurt too badly.

After that, I took the tin away. I beat it until I was exhausted and miserable. Then Harris took it.

We beat it until it was long and thin. We beat it until it was square. We hit it with the wood until it was every shape there is – but we could not make a hole in it. Then George tried, and he knocked it into a shape which was strange, and terrible, and ugly. It frightened him, and he threw away the piece of wood. Then the three of us sat round that tin on the grass, and we looked at it.

There was one big line across the top of the tin that looked like a mouth. It seemed to be laughing at us, and this made us very angry. So Harris ran at it, and picked it up. He threw it, as hard as he could, into the middle of the river. As it went down into the water, we shouted awful things at it. Then we got into the boat, and we left that place, and did not stop until we reached Maidenhead.

We went through Maidenhead quickly, but, after that, we travelled along more slowly. We stopped for tea just before we got to Cookham. By the time we got through the lock it was evening.

It was a bit windy, and someone had made a mistake

We beat that tin into every shape there is - but we could not make a hole in it.

because the wind was behind us. That does not usually happen. But that afternoon the wind actually helped us on our way, and the boat moved quite fast.

There were no other people on the river, except for three old men. They were sitting in a boat, and they were fishing. As we got nearer, we could see that they were old. They were also quite serious, because they were watching their fishing-lines very carefully. The sun was going down, and it threw a red light across the water. It was very beautiful, and we felt that we were sailing into some strange land.

We did not sail into some strange land. We went straight into that boat with the three old men in it. At first, we did not know what had happened. But then, from the words which rose on the evening air, we understood that we were near people. We also understood that those people were not happy. We had knocked those three old men from their seats, and they were all lying on the bottom of their boat. They were trying to stand up and they were picking fish off themselves. As they worked, they shouted unkind things about us – not just the usual things, but special things about us, and about our families.

Harris called out, 'You ought to be pleased that something so exciting has happened to you!' He added that he was very unhappy to hear men of their age use those bad words.

But the three old men did not seem to agree with Harris.

At Marlow we left the boat near the bridge, and we went to spend the night in a hotel.

Chapter 12

Montmorency and the cat

On Monday morning, we got up quite early and we went to swim before breakfast. On the way back, Montmorency behaved very stupidly.

The only thing that Montmorency and I disagree about is cats. I like cats. Montmorency does not.

When I meet a cat, I say hello to it. Then I bend down and I stroke it gently, behind the ears and along the side of its head. The cat likes this. It puts its tail up and it pushes itself against my legs. And there is love and peace. When Montmorency meets a cat, everybody knows about it, and a lot of bad words are used.

I do not really blame Montmorency (usually I just hit him, or throw stones at him), because dogs are like that. They hate cats. But that morning, Montmorency wished that he had not argued with a cat.

As we were coming back from the river, a cat ran out from one of the houses, and it began to walk across the road. Montmorency saw the cat, gave a shout of real happiness, and ran after it.

It was a big, black cat. I have never seen a bigger cat. It had lost half its tail and one of its ears, but it looked calm and happy.

Montmorency and the cat did not speak, of course, but it was easy to imagine their conversation.

Montmorency ran at that cat as fast as he could, but the cat did not hurry. It did not seem to understand that its life was in danger. It walked on quietly until the enemy was near it. Then it turned and sat down in the middle of the road. It looked at Montmorency in a quiet way, and it seemed to say,

'Yes? You want me?'

Montmorency is quite a brave dog, but there was something in the way the cat looked at him. It frightened him. He stopped suddenly, and he looked at the cat. They did not speak, of course, but it was easy to imagine their conversation.

THE CAT: Can I do anything for you?

MONTMORENCY: No . . . no, thanks.

THE CAT: Do please tell me if there is something you want, won't you?

MONTMORENCY *(who moves backwards down the road)*: Oh, no. Not at all . . . certainly . . . I . . . I'm afraid I've made a mistake. I thought I knew you . . . I'm sorry.

THE CAT: Not at all. Are you quite sure you don't want anything now?

MONTMORENCY *(who continues to move back)*: Not at all . . . thanks . . . not at all . . . very kind of you . . . Good morning.

THE CAT: Good morning.

Then the cat stood up and continued along the road. Montmorency, with his tail between his legs, walked behind us. He hoped that nobody would notice him.

Now, if you say 'Cats!' to Montmorency, he looks up at you, and his eyes beg you, 'No, please!'

After this we did our shopping, went back to the boat, and moved off along the river again. However, at Hambledon lock, we found that we had no water. So we went to ask the lock-keeper for some. George spoke for us. He said, 'Oh, please, could you give us a little water?'

'Of course,' the old man replied. 'Just take what you want and leave the rest.'

'Thank you very much,' George said, and he looked round. 'But where is it?'

'It's where it always is, my boy,' the lock-keeper answered. 'It's behind you.'

George looked round again. 'I can't see it,' he said.

'Why? Where are your eyes?' the man said, and he turned George towards the river.

'Oh!' George cried. 'But we can't drink the river, you know.'

'No, but you can drink some of it,' the old man replied. 'That's what I've drunk for fifteen years.'

We got some water from another house.

After we had got our water, we went on towards Wargrave, but before we got there, we stopped for lunch.

We were sitting in a field near the river, and we were just going to start eating. Harris was preparing the food, and George and I were waiting with our plates.

'Have you got a spoon?' Harris asked. 'I need a spoon.'

The basket was behind us, and George and I both turned to get a spoon. It took about five seconds. When we looked back again, Harris and the food had gone. It was an open field, and there were no trees. There was nowhere to hide. He had not fallen in the river, because we were between him and the water.

George and I looked round. Then we looked at each other. Harris had gone – disappeared! Sadly, we looked again at the place where Harris and the food had been. And then, to our horror, we saw Harris's head – and only his head – in the grass. The face was very red and very angry.

George was the first to speak.

'Say something!' he cried. 'Are you alive or dead? Where is the rest of you?'

'Oh, don't be so stupid!' Harris's head said. 'It's your fault. You made me sit there. You did it to annoy me! Here, take the food!'

And from the middle of the grass the food appeared, and then Harris came out, dirty and wet.

Harris had not known that he had been sitting on the edge of a hole. The grass had hidden it. Then, suddenly, he had fallen backwards into it. He said he had not known what was happening to him. He thought, at first, that it was the end of the world.

Harris still believes that George and I planned it.

Chapter 13

Harris and the swans

After lunch, we moved on to Wargrave and Shiplake, and then to Sonning. We got out of the boat there, and we walked about for an hour or more. It was too late then to go on past Reading, so we decided to go back to one of the Shiplake islands. We would spend the night there.

When we had tied the boat up by one of the islands, it was still early. George said it would be a good idea to have a really excellent supper. He said we could use all kinds of things, and all the bits of food we had left. We could make it really interesting, and we could put everything into one big pan together. George said he would show us how to do it.

We liked this idea, so George collected wood to make a fire. Harris and I started to prepare the potatoes. This became a very big job. We began quite happily. However, by the time we had finished our first potato, we were feeling very miserable. There was almost no potato left. George came and looked at it.

'Oh, that's no good. You've done it wrong! Do it like this!' he said.

We worked very hard for twenty-five minutes. At the end of that time we had done four potatoes. We refused to continue.

George said it was stupid to have only four potatoes, so we washed about six more. Then we put them in the pan without doing anything else to them. We also put in some carrots and other vegetables. But George looked at it, and he said there was not enough. So then we got out both the food baskets. We took out all the bits of things that were left, and we put them in, too. In fact, we put in everything we could find. I remember that Montmorency watched all this, and he looked very thoughtful. Then he walked away. He came back a few minutes later with a dead rat in his mouth. He wanted to give it to us for the meal. We did not know if he really wanted to put it in the pan, or if he wanted to tell us what he thought about the meal. Harris said he thought it would be all right to put the rat in. However, George did not want to try anything new.

It was a very good meal. It was different from other meals. The potatoes were a bit hard, but we had good teeth, so it did not really matter.

After supper Harris was rather disagreeable – I think it was the meal which caused this. He is not used to such rich food. George and I decided to go for a walk in Henley, but we left Harris in the boat. He said he was going to have a glass of whisky, smoke his pipe, and then get the boat ready for the night. We were on an island, so when we came back we would shout from the river bank. Then Harris would come in the boat and get us. When we left, we said to him, 'Don't go to sleep!'

Henley was very busy, and we met quite a lot of people

we knew in town. The time passed very quickly. When we started off on our long walk back, it was eleven o'clock.

It was a dark and miserable night. It was quite cold, and it was raining a bit. We walked through the dark, silent fields, and we talked quietly to each other. We wondered if we were going the right way. We thought of our nice, warm, comfortable boat. We thought of Harris, and Montmorency, and the whisky – and we wished that we were there.

We imagined that we were inside our warm little boat, tired and a little hungry, with the dark, miserable river outside. We could see ourselves – we were sitting down to supper there; we were passing cold meat and thick pieces of bread to each other. We could hear the happy sounds of our knives and our laughing voices. We hurried to make it real.

After some time, we found the river, and that made us happy. We knew that we were going the right way. We passed Shiplake at a quarter to twelve, and then George said, quite slowly. 'You don't remember which island it was, do you?'

'No, I don't,' I replied, and I began to think carefully. 'How many are there?'

'Only four,' George answered. 'It'll be all right, if Harris is awake.'

'And if he isn't awake?' I asked.

But we decided not to think about that.

When we arrived opposite the first island, we shouted, but there was no answer. So we went to the second island, and we tried there. The result was the same.

'Oh, I remember now,' George said. 'It was the third one.'

And, full of hope, we ran to the third one, and we called out. There was no answer.

It was now becoming serious. It was after midnight. The hotels were all full, and we could not go round all the houses and knock on doors at midnight! George said that perhaps we could go back to Henley, find a policeman and hit him. He would arrest us and take us to a police station, and then we would have somewhere to sleep. But then we thought, 'Perhaps he won't arrest us. Perhaps he'll just hit us, too!' We could not fight policemen all night.

We tried the fourth island, but there was still no reply. It was raining hard now, and it was not going to stop. We were very cold, and wet, and miserable. We began to wonder if there were only four islands, or if we were on the wrong bit of the river. Everything looked strange and different in the darkness.

Just when we had lost all hope, I suddenly saw a strange light. It was over by the trees, on the opposite side of the river. I shouted as loudly as I could.

We waited in silence for a moment, and then (Oh, how happy we were!) we heard Montmorency bark.

We continued to shout for about five minutes, and then we saw the lights of the boat. It was coming towards us slowly. We heard Harris's sleepy voice. He was asking where we were.

Harris seemed very strange. It was more than tiredness. He brought the boat to our side of the river. He stopped, at a place where we could not get into the boat, and then immediately he fell asleep.

We had to scream and yell to wake him up again. At last we did wake him up, and we got into the boat.

Harris looked very sad. In fact, he looked like a man who had had a lot of trouble. We asked him if anything had happened, and he said, 'Swans!'

We had left the boat near a swan's nest, and, soon after George and I had left, Mrs Swan came back. She started to shout at Harris. However, Harris managed to chase her away, and she went to fetch her husband. Harris said he had had quite a hard battle with these two swans. But he had fought bravely and, in the end, he defeated them.

Half an hour later they returned – with eighteen more swans. There was another terrible battle. Harris said the swans had tried to pull him and Montmorency from the boat and drown them. But, once again, Harris fought bravely, for four hours, and he had killed them all. Then they had all swum away to die.

'How many swans did you say there were?' George asked.

'Thirty-two,' Harris replied, sleepily.

'You said eighteen before,' George said.

'No, I didn't,' Harris answered. 'I said twelve. Do you think I can't count?'

We never discovered what had really happened. We asked Harris about it the next morning, but he said, 'What swans?' And he seemed to think that George and I had been dreaming.

Harris said that he had had a terrible battle with the swans.

Oh, how wonderful it was to be in the boat again! We ate a very good supper, and then we thought we would have some whisky. But we could not find it. We asked Harris what he had done with it, but he did not seem to understand. The expression on Montmorency's face told us that he knew something, but he said nothing.

I slept well that night, although Harris did wake me up ten times or more. He was looking for his clothes. He seemed to be worrying about his clothes all night.

Twice he made George and me get up, because he wanted to see if we were lying on his trousers. George got quite angry the second time.

'Whatever do you want your trousers for? It's the middle of the night!' he cried. 'Why don't you lie down and go to sleep?'

The next time I woke up Harris said he could not find his shoes. And I can remember that once he pushed me over onto my side. 'Wherever can that umbrella be?' he was saying.

Chapter 14

Work, washing, and fishing

We woke up late the next morning, and it was about ten o'clock when we moved off. We had already decided that we wanted to make this a good day's journey.

We agreed that we would row, and not tow, the boat. Harris said that George and I should row, and he would steer. I did not like this idea at all. I said that he and George should row, so that I could rest a little. I thought that I was doing too much of the work on this trip. I was beginning to feel strongly about it.

I always think that I am doing too much work. It is not because I do not like work. I do like it. I find it very interesting. I can sit and look at it for hours. You cannot give me too much work. I like to collect it. My study is full of it.

And I am very careful with my work, too. Why, some of the work in my study has been there for years, and it has not got dirty or anything. That is because I take care of it.

However, although I love work, I do not want to take other people's work from them. But I get it without asking for it, and this worries me.

George says that I should not worry about it. In fact, he thinks that perhaps I should have more work. However, I expect he only says that to make me feel better.

In a boat, I have noticed that each person thinks that he is doing all the work. Harris's idea was that both George and I had let him do all the work. George said that Harris never did anything except eat and sleep. He, George, had done all the work. He said that he had never met such lazy people as Harris and me.

That amused Harris.

'George! Work!' he laughed. 'If George worked for half an hour, it would kill him. Have you ever seen George work?' he added, and he turned to me.

I agreed with Harris that I had never seen George work.

'Well, how can you know?' George answered Harris. 'You're always asleep. Have you ever seen Harris awake, except at meal times?' George asked me.

I had to tell the truth and agree with George. Harris had done very little work in the boat.

'Oh, come on! I've done more than old J., anyway,' Harris replied.

'Well, it would be difficult to do less,' George added.

'Oh, him, he thinks he's a passenger and doesn't need to work!' Harris said.

And that was how grateful they were to me, after I had brought them and their old boat all the way up from Kingston; after I had organized everything for them; and after I had taken care of them!

Finally, we decided that Harris and George would row until we got past Reading, and then I would tow the boat from there.

We reached Reading at about eleven o'clock. We did not stay long, though, because the river is dirty there. However, after that it becomes very beautiful. Goring, on the left, and Streatley, on the right, are both very pretty places. Earlier, we had decided to go on to Wallingford that day, but the river was lovely at Streatley. We left our boat at the bridge, and we went into the village. We had lunch at a little pub, and Montmorency enjoyed that.

We stayed at Streatley for two days, and we took our clothes to be washed. We had tried to wash them ourselves, in the river, and George had told us what to do. This was not a success! Before we washed them, they were very, very dirty, but we could just wear them. After we had washed them, they were worse than before. However, the river between Reading and Henley was cleaner because we had taken all the dirt from it, and we had washed it into our clothes. The woman who washed them at Streatley made us pay three times the usual price.

We paid her, and did not say a word about the cost.

The river near Streatley and Goring is excellent for fishing. You can sit and fish there all day.

Some people do sit and fish all day. They never catch any fish, of course. You may catch a dead cat or two, but you will not catch any fish. When you go for a walk by the river, the fish come and stand half out of the water, with their mouths open for bread. And if you go swimming, they all come and stare at you and get in your way. But you cannot catch them.

The fish come and stand half out of the water, with their mouths open for bread.

On the second evening, George and I and Montmorency (I do not know where Harris was) went for a walk to Wallingford. On the way back to the boat, we stopped at a little pub, by the river.

We went in and sat down. There was an old man there. He was smoking a pipe, and we began to talk to him.

He told us that it had been a fine day today, and we told him that it had been a fine day yesterday. Then we all told each other that we thought it would be a fine day tomorrow.

We told him that we were on holiday on the river, and that we were going to leave the next day. Then we stopped talking for a few minutes, and we began to look round the room. We noticed a glass case on the wall. In it there was a very big fish.

The old man saw that we were looking at this fish.

'Ah,' he said, 'that's a big fish, isn't it?'

'Yes, it is,' I replied.

'Yes,' the old man continued, 'it was sixteen years ago. I caught him just by the bridge.'

'Did you, really?' George asked.

'Yes,' the man answered. 'They told me he was in the river. I said I'd catch him, and I did. You don't see many fish as big as that one now. Well, goodnight, then.' And he went out.

After that, we could not take our eyes off the fish. It really was a fine fish. We were still looking at it when another man came in. He had a glass of beer in his hand, and he also looked at the fish.

'That's a fine, big fish, isn't it?' George said to him.

'Ah, yes,' the man replied. He drank some of his beer, and then he added, 'Perhaps you weren't here when it was caught?'

'No,' we said, and we explained that we did not live there. We said that we were only there on holiday.

'Ah, well,' the man went on, 'it was nearly five years ago that I caught that fish.'

'Oh, did you catch it then?' I asked.

'Yes,' he replied. 'I caught him by the lock . . . Well, goodnight to you.'

Five minutes later a third man came in and described how he had caught the fish, early one morning. He left, and another man came in and sat down by the window.

Nobody spoke for some time. Then George turned to the man and said, 'Excuse me, I hope you don't mind, but my friend and I, who are only on holiday here, would like to ask you a question. Could you tell us how you caught that fish?'

'Who told you that I caught that fish?' he asked.

We said that nobody had told us. We just felt that he was the man who had caught it.

'Well, that's very strange,' he answered, with a little laugh. 'You're right. I did catch it.' And he went on to tell us how he had done it, and that it had taken him half an hour to land it.

When he left, the landlord came in to talk to us. We told him the different stories we had heard about his fish. He was very amused and we all laughed about it. And then he told us the real story of the fish.

He said that he had caught it himself, years ago, when he was a boy. It was a lovely, sunny afternoon, and instead of going to school, he went fishing. That was when he caught the fish. Everyone thought he was very clever. Even his teacher thought he had done well and did not punish him.

He had to go out of the room just then, and we turned to look at the fish again. George became very excited about it, and he climbed up onto a chair to see it better.

And then George fell, and he caught hold of the glass case to save himself. It came down, with George and the chair on top of it.

'Is the fish all right?' I cried.

'I hope so,' George said. He stood up carefully and looked round. But the fish was lying on the floor – in a thousand pieces!

It was not a real fish.

Chapter 15

On to Oxford

We left Streatley early the next morning. We were going to Culham, and we wanted to spend the night there. Between Streatley and Wallingford the river is not very interesting. Then from Cleeve there is quite a long piece of the river which has no locks. Most people are pleased about this because it makes everything much easier, but I quite like locks, myself. I remember that George and I nearly had an accident in a lock once . . .

It was a lovely day, and there were a lot of boats in the lock. Someone was taking a photograph of us all, and the photographer was hoping to sell the picture to the people in the lock. I did not see the photographer at first, but suddenly George started to brush his trousers, and he fixed his hair and put on his hat. Then he sat down with a kind, but sad, expression on his face, and he tried to hide his feet.

My first idea was that he had seen a girl that he knew, and I looked round to see who it was. Everybody in the lock had stopped moving and they all had fixed expressions on their faces. All the girls were smiling prettily, and all the men were trying to look brave and handsome.

Then I saw the photographer and at once I understood. I wondered if I would be in time. Our boat was the first one in the lock, so I must look nice for the man's photograph.

So I turned round quickly and stood in the front of the boat. I arranged my hair carefully, and I tried to make myself look strong and interesting.

We stood and waited for the important moment when the man would actually take the photograph. Just then, someone behind me called out,

'Hi! Look at your nose!'

I could not turn round to see whose nose it was, but I had a quick look at George's nose. It seemed to be all right. I tried to look at my own nose, and that seemed to be all right, too.

'Look at your nose, you stupid fool!' the voice cried again, more loudly this time.

And then another voice called, 'Push your nose out! You two, with the dog!'

We could not turn round because the man was just going to take the photograph. Was it us they were calling to? What was the matter with our noses? Why did they want us to push them out?

But now everybody in the lock started shouting, and a very loud, deep voice from the back called, 'Look at your boat! You, in the red and black caps! If you don't do something quickly, there'll be two dead bodies in that photograph!'

We looked then, and we saw that the nose of our boat was caught in the wooden gate at the front of

Everybody in the lock started shouting at us, 'Push your nose out!'

the lock. The water was rising, and our boat was beginning to turn over. Quickly, we pushed hard against the side of the lock, to move the boat. The boat did move, and George and I fell over on our backs.

We did not come out well in that photograph because the man took it just as we fell over. We had expressions of 'Where am I?' and 'What's happened?' on our faces, and we were waving our feet about wildly. In fact, our feet nearly filled the photograph. You could not see much else.

Nobody bought the photographs. They said they did not want photographs of our feet. The photographer was not very pleased . . .

We passed Wallingford and Dorchester, and we spent the night at Clifton Hampden, which is a very pretty little village.

The next morning we were up early, because we wanted to be in Oxford by the afternoon. By half past eight we had finished breakfast and we were through Clifton lock. At half past twelve we went through Iffley lock.

From there to Oxford is the most difficult part of the river. First the river carries you to the right, then to the left; then it takes you out into the middle and turns you round three times. We got in the way of a lot of other boats; a lot of other boats got in our way – and a lot of bad words were used.

However, at Oxford we had two good days. There are a lot of dogs in the town. Montmorency had eleven fights on the first day and fourteen on the second. This made him very happy.

If you are thinking of taking a trip on the river, and you are going to start from Oxford, take your own boat (unless you can take someone else's without being discovered). The boats that you can hire on the Thames above Marlow are all right: they do not let too much water in, and they have seats and things. But they are not really boats which you want people to see. The person who hires one of these boats is the kind of person who likes to stay under the trees. He likes to travel early in the morning or late at night, when there are not many people about to look at him. When he sees someone he knows, he gets out of the boat and hides behind a tree. I remember that some friends and I hired one of these boats one summer . . .

We had written to ask for a boat, and, when we arrived at the boathouse, we gave our names. The man said, 'Oh, yes.' And then he called out to another man, 'Jim, fetch "The Queen of the Thames".'

Five minutes later, Jim came back with a very old piece of wood. He had clearly just dug it up from a hole in the ground. When he dug it up, he had damaged it very badly.

We asked Jim what it was.

'It's "The Queen of the Thames",' he answered.

We laughed at this, and then one of us said, 'All right. Now go and fetch the real boat.'

They said that this was the real boat . . .

Chapter 16

The journey home

We left Oxford on the third day, to go back home. The weather changed, and, when we left Oxford, it was raining. It continued to rain, not heavily, but all the time.

When the sun is shining, the river turns everything into a golden dream. But when it rains, the river is brown and miserable.

It rained all day, and, at first, we pretended we were enjoying it. We said that it was a nice change. We added that it was good to see the river in all kinds of weather. Harris and I sang a song about how good it was to be free and to be able to enjoy the sun and the rain.

George thought it was much more serious, and he put up the umbrella.

Before lunch, he put the cover on the boat, and it stayed there all afternoon. We just left a little hole, so that we could see out. We stopped for the night, just before Day's lock, and I cannot say that we spent a happy evening.

The rain came down without stopping. Everything in the boat was wet. Supper was not a success. We were all tired of cold meat, and we talked about our favourite foods. When we passed the cold meat to Montmorency, he refused our offer. He went and sat at the other end of the boat, alone.

The rain came down without stopping.
Everything in the boat was wet.

We played cards after supper. We played for about an hour and a half, and George won ten pence. Harris and I lost five pence each. We decided to stop then, because the game was getting too exciting.

After that we had some whisky, and we sat and talked. George told us about a man he had known. This man had slept on the river, in a wet boat, like ours, and it had made him very ill. Ten days later, the poor man died, in great pain. George said he was quite a young man, so it was very sad.

Then Harris remembered one of his friends who had camped out on a wet night. When he woke up the next morning, he was in great pain, and he was never able to walk again.

So then, of course, we began to talk about other illnesses. Harris said it would be very serious if one of us became ill because we were a long way from a doctor.

After this we really needed something to make us feel a bit happier, so George sang to us. That really made us cry.

After that we could think of nothing else to do, so we went to bed. Well . . . we undressed and we lay down in the boat. We tried to go to sleep but it was four hours before we did so. At five o'clock we all woke up again, so we got up and had breakfast.

The second day was the same as the first. It rained all day. We sat in our raincoats under the cover, and we travelled slowly along the river. I did try to sing again, but it was not a success.

However, we all agreed that we should continue our trip.

We had come to enjoy ourselves for a fortnight on the river, and we were going to finish the trip. If it killed us – well, that would be a sad thing for our friends and families, but we would not give in to the weather.

'It's only two more days,' Harris said, 'and we are young and strong. Perhaps we'll be all right.'

At about four o'clock we began to discuss our plans for that evening. We were a little past Goring then, and we decided to go on to Pangbourne and spend the night there.

'Another happy evening,' George said.

We sat and thought about it. We would be in Pangbourne by five o'clock. We would finish our dinner by half past six. After that we could walk about the village in the rain, or we could sit in a dark little pub.

'It would be more interesting to go to the Alhambra Theatre in London,' Harris said, and he looked out at the sky.

'With supper afterwards at that little French restaurant,' I added.

'Yes, I'm almost sorry we've decided to stay on the boat,' Harris said. Then we were silent for a time.

'I know we've decided to stay and die on this boat,' George said, 'but there is a train which leaves Pangbourne soon after five o'clock. We could be in London in time to get something to eat, and afterwards we could go on to the theatre.'

Nobody said a word. We looked at each other, and we all felt badly about it. We did not speak, but we got out the bag.

We looked up the river, and down the river. There was nobody there.

Twenty minutes later, three figures and an ashamed dog quietly left the nearest boathouse, and went towards the station.

We had told the boatman a lie. We had asked him to take care of the boat for us until nine o'clock the next morning. We said we would come back for it then. However, if (only 'if') something happened to stop us from coming back, then we would write to him.

We reached Paddington station at seven o'clock, and we drove straight to the restaurant. We had a light meal and left Montmorency there. Then we went to the theatre. For some reason everybody stared at us, and this made us very happy. Perhaps it was because of our interesting clothes, or because we looked so healthy.

Afterwards we went back to the restaurant, where supper was waiting for us.

We really did enjoy that supper. For ten days we had lived on cold meat and bread, and not much else. We ate and drank without speaking, and then we sat back and rested. We felt good, and thoughtful, and kind.

Then Harris, who was sitting next to the window, pulled back the curtain and looked out into the street. It was still raining, and it was dark and very wet. One or two people hurried past. The rain was running from their umbrellas, and the women were holding up their long skirts.

Harris picked up his glass.

'Well,' he said, 'we've had a good trip, and I'm very grateful to Old Father Thames. But I think we were right to give up and come back. Here's to Three Men well out of a Boat!'

And Montmorency stood on his back legs in front of the window, looked out into the night, and gave a short bark to show that he agreed.

GLOSSARY

aground *(adv)* touching the bottom of the river in shallow water

bank (**river**) the ground on each side of a river

bark *(n)* the short quick sound that a dog makes

bedclothes the blankets and sheets on a bed

blow *(n)* hitting someone or something hard

camp *(v)* to sleep outside in the open air or in tents

cap *(n)* a kind of hat worn by men

case a kind of box with glass in the front

fool *(n)* a very stupid person

hammer *(n)* a piece of wood with a heavy metal head used for hitting things

hedge *(n)* a 'wall' of small trees which have been planted together

housekeeper a person who takes care of a house

keeper a person who takes care of something

landlord the owner of a pub

lock *(n)* a place on a river between gates where boats are raised or lowered to a different level

lock-keeper a person who looks after a lock on a river

maze lots of high hedges with narrow paths between them; people have to find their way in and out, and usually get lost

nail *(n)* a small thin piece of metal with a sharp end

nest *(n)* a place that a bird makes to have its eggs

nose *(n)* (in this story) the front of a boat

piano a large musical instrument with black and white keys that you press to make music

rat a little grey animal with a long tail

rope   very thick, strong string, used for tying things

splash *(v)*   to make water fly about and make things wet

steer   to turn a wheel or handle to guide a boat, car, etc.

stick (past tense **stuck**)   to fix or fasten one thing to another thing

stove   a small oil cooker, used for cooking outdoors

stroke *(v)*   to move the hand gently across something, again and again

swan   a big white bird with a long neck

symptom   a sign of illness

teapot   a pot in which tea is made

tent   a small house made of cloth over poles

tin   a metal container for keeping foods

tin-opener   the thing used to cut open a tin

tow   to pull a boat, car, etc. along behind you with a rope

yell *(v)*   to shout very loudly

Three Men in a Boat

ACTIVITIES

Before Reading

1 **Read the back cover and the story introduction on the first page of the book. Are these sentences true (T) or false (F)?**

1 The three friends are going to have a holiday on a boat.

2 They are going to take the boat out to sea.

3 Their adventures are going to be funny.

4 This story was written in the 1990s.

5 Montmorency is a cat.

6 J is a young man.

2 **What is going to happen in the story? Do you know, or can you guess? For each sentence, circle Y (Yes), N (No) or P (Perhaps).**

The three friends . . .

1 fall in the river. Y/N/P

2 lose the tin-opener. Y/N/P

3 cook their own meals. Y/N/P

4 get wet. Y/N/P

5 argue a lot. Y/N/P

6 tell stories. Y/N/P

7 go fishing. Y/N/P

8 wash their own clothes. Y/N/P

9 meet dangerous animals. Y/N/P

10 go swimming. Y/N/P

11 find a lot of money. Y/N/P

12 get arrested. Y/N/P

13 lose the boat. Y/N/P

14 play cards. Y/N/P

15 watch television. Y/N/P

Montmorency . . .

16 fights a cat. Y/N/P

17 gets lost. Y/N/P

18 falls in the river. Y/N/P

19 runs away. Y/N/P

20 kills another dog. Y/N/P

3 **Which of the following things do the friends pack for their holiday? Can you guess? Underline the things that they pack. Add ten more useful things to the list.**

clothes, a tent, toothbrushes, a tin-opener, whisky, fruit, umbrellas, eggs, a teapot, a map, a radio, a telephone

4 **Have you ever been on holiday on a boat or in a tent? What do you think are the good things and the bad things about this kind of holiday?**

ACTIVITIES

While Reading

Read Chapters 1 to 3. Are these sentences true (T) or false (F)? Rewrite the false ones with the correct information.

1 The three friends all said that they felt ill.
2 Harris wanted to go to the country.
3 Montmorency liked the idea of a holiday on the river.
4 Harris and J were going to take the boat from Kingston to Chertsey.
5 George had to stay at work until Saturday afternoon.
6 The friends decided to sleep in hotels every night.
7 Montmorency had once killed a cat.
8 George said that a tent was easier than a cover over the boat.

Read Chapters 4 to 6. Then answer these questions.

Who . . .
1 . . . couldn't find his toothbrush?
2 . . . packed a pan on top of a tomato?
3 . . . stepped on the butter?
4 . . . ran away with the teaspoons?
5 . . . woke J up the next morning?
6 . . . read the weather report and then went to work?
7 . . . waited twenty minutes for a taxi?
8 . . . had once got lost in Hampton Court maze?

Read Chapters 7 and 8. Here are some untrue sentences. Rewrite them with the correct information.

1 Harris and J visited the church at Hampton.
2 Harris thought that George worked hard.
3 Harris thought that water was good for people.
4 Harris fell into the river.
5 J's cap fell into the river.
6 They met George at Sunbury lock.
7 The lock-keeper seemed pleased that no one had fallen in.
8 Harris pulled the boat to Penton Hook.

Read Chapters 9 and 10, and then put these sentences in the correct order.

1 Then they went to bed.
2 After that, they put the water on the stove for tea.
3 J fell into the river.
4 The friends tied their boat to a tree.
5 Unfortunately, George and Harris got caught under the cover.
6 George told a funny story about his watch.
7 At last, they had supper.
8 Then he dropped George's shirt into the water.
9 George and J woke up at six o'clock the next morning.
10 Then they fixed the pieces of metal for the cover.
11 After supper, George told a funny story about his father.

Read Chapters 11 and 12, and then answer these questions.

Why . . .

1 . . . didn't the friends like the Black Horse?
2 . . . couldn't they open the tin of fruit?
3 . . . were the three old men angry with the friends?
4 . . . didn't Montmorency fight the black cat?
5 . . . did Harris disappear?

Read Chapters 13 to 15. Choose the best question-word for these questions, and then answer them.

How many / What / Why

1 . . . did George and J decide to do after supper?
2 . . . islands were there in the river?
3 . . . did George want to find a policeman and hit him?
4 . . . swans did Harris fight?
5 . . . did Harris do with the whisky?
6 . . . happened to their clothes when they washed them?
7 . . . people said that they had caught the fish in the glass case?
8 . . . did George start to brush his trousers in the lock?

Before you read Chapter 16, can you guess what happens? Choose one answer each time.

1 a) It starts to rain.
   b) The weather is fine.
2 a) The friends go back to London by boat.
   b) The friends leave the boat and go home by train.

After Reading

1 **Match these halves of sentences and put them in the correct order to tell the story of the night in Datchet. Use these words to join your sentences.**

and / and / because / because / but / but / that / that

1 Then George decided to ask for a room at the Black Horse,

2 _____ the friends were looking for somewhere to stay in Datchet.

3 _____ the man said that they didn't have any beds.

4 _____ it didn't have roses round the door.

5 _____ they were all full.

6 At the Travellers' Rest, the lady said

7 It was one Saturday in August

8 Harris didn't like the second one

9 At last, a little boy told them

10 _____ of the man standing by the front door.

11 _____ they were never so difficult about hotels again!

12 _____ she had already sent away fourteen people.

13 The three friends had to sleep in two beds

14 J didn't like the first hotel

15 After that, the friends tried three houses and a shop,

16 _____ his mother could give them a room.

2 **Imagine that Montmorency told another dog about the holiday. Fill in the gaps in his story with a verb or a preposition. (Use one word in each gap.)**

I didn't want to go _____ holiday on the river because I knew that there was nothing to _____. I don't _____ peace and quiet, I like to have fights _____ other dogs. But I enjoyed the packing because I _____ that the oranges were rats and I _____ three _____ them. The holiday wasn't very interesting; I just sat _____ the boat while the others rowed or _____ it with a rope. And one day in Marlow I _____ a terrible experience. I _____ a cat walking across the road. It was big and black, and I _____ that I could frighten it _____ running at it. This is what I usually do with cats; I hate them. But this cat just sat down _____ the middle of the road and looked _____ me. There was something about it that _____ me. So I moved back with my tail _____ my legs and hid _____ J. Oxford was all right, because there were a lot of dogs in the town. I had eleven fights _____ the first day and fourteen _____ the second. I really _____ myself! The food on this holiday wasn't very good. One night I _____ myself on the pan when Harris was cooking eggs, and another night they _____ a strange supper _____ all the bits of food they had left over. I tried to give them a dead rat to put in the pan but they didn't _____ it. I was very happy when we went back _____ London and _____ dinner at a restaurant, I can tell you.

3 **Complete these descriptions of the three friends. Write the correct name in the first gap, and then fill in the other gaps using as many words as you like.**

1 _____ likes to tell everybody _____. Once, he was in the maze at Hampton Court and he met some people who _____. He told them that he knew the way, so _____. But he got lost and the people _____. He also says that he is good _____. But when he tried to cook some eggs for breakfast, _____. He likes to drink whisky and one night, he drank a whole bottle. After that, he told the others _____.

2 _____ works in a bank, but he is always _____. He hates _____ in the morning, but once, he got up in the middle of the night because _____. He is very lazy, and he told a story about how he made a young man and a young woman _____. One night he made an excellent supper with _____. Another evening, he was in a pub and he climbed up onto a chair to look at a fish in a glass case, but _____.

3 _____ thinks that he is good _____. But when he packed the clothes, _____. On the first morning of the holiday, he woke up early and went down to the edge of the river to _____, but _____. Then, when he tried to put his shirt on, _____. He was very angry, until he noticed that _____.

4 The friends tell a lot of stories. Match the titles below with the stories that begin on these pages.

page 1, page 5, page 7, page 12, page 20, page 22, page 30, page 31, page 38, page 40, page 48, page 74, page 78

How girls tow a boat	Lost in the maze
No room in Datchet	A visit to the library
Sleeping in a tent	The dangers of a sea trip
Hiring a boat	The photograph
Aunt Mary is lost	Two men in one bed
Uncle Podger and the picture	Weather reports
When George got up early	

5 These sentences describe two scenes from the book. Separate the two scenes and put them in the correct order. There are eight sentences for each one.

1 This means that they pull the boat much too fast.
2 Two of you try to put it up, but it is very heavy and falls on top of you.
3 Soon they stop again, because they want their hats or because they have seen a cow.
4 But then you get your side up and begin to tie the ropes to the ground.
5 You always need three girls to tow a boat.
6 So you pull your side hard, and pull out all the ropes on his side.

7 When they do that, the boat goes out into the middle of the river and starts to turn round.

8 Finally, the tent falls down and you have to start again.

9 After a few minutes, they get tired of running and stop suddenly.

10 It is almost impossible to put up a tent in the rain.

11 So you have to shout at them, 'Keep the boat moving!', and they start pulling again.

12 And then he gives a violent pull and your side comes out too.

13 When they finally get the rope straight, they always start by running.

14 So you follow each other round and round and shout at each other.

15 Just then, the other man pulls from his side and destroys all your hard work.

16 They usually begin by tying themselves up in the rope.

6 **The book makes us laugh because the characters say things that we know are not true. Find five examples, and then write sentences telling the truth. Use some of these words.**

heart, illness, seasick, work, whisky, packing, water, eggs, swans, fish

Example: 'It is not because I do not like work. I do like it. I find it very interesting. I can sit and look at it for hours.'
The truth: J does not like work. He is lazy and will avoid doing any work for as long as he possibly can.

ABOUT THE AUTHOR

Jerome Klapka Jerome was born in 1859 and grew up in east London, the son of an unsuccessful shopkeeper. When he was fourteen, he took a job selling railway tickets and later became a teacher. He then became an actor and in 1885 he published his first book, which was a collection of funny stories about the theatre.

But he did not become well known until 1889, when he wrote *Three Men in a Boat*, about his own experiences with his friends on the River Thames. *Three Men in a Boat* has continued to make people laugh for over a hundred years because of its 'banana-skin' humour. We find it funny when people step on a banana skin in the street and fall over; in the same way, we recognize the little everyday problems and accidents that Jerome describes in so much detail.

In 1892, Jerome and some friends began a magazine, *The Idler*, where they published work by writers like Mark Twain and W. W. Jacobs. In 1900, Jerome wrote another book, *Three Men on the Bummel*, where the same three friends go on a trip to Germany, and he also wrote many successful plays.

During the First World War, Jerome worked as an ambulance driver in France, and after the war, he continued writing. He always loved the Thames and lived for many years near Ewelme in Oxfordshire, not far from the river that he described in *Three Men in a Boat*. He died in 1927.

ABOUT BOOKWORMS

OXFORD BOOKWORMS LIBRARY

Classics • True Stories • Fantasy & Horror • Human Interest
Crime & Mystery • Thriller & Adventure

The OXFORD BOOKWORMS LIBRARY offers a wide range of original and adapted stories, both classic and modern, which take learners from elementary to advanced level through six carefully graded language stages:

Stage 1 (400 headwords)	**Stage 4** (1400 headwords)
Stage 2 (700 headwords)	**Stage 5** (1800 headwords)
Stage 3 (1000 headwords)	**Stage 6** (2500 headwords)

More than fifty titles are also available on cassette, and there are many titles at Stages 1 to 4 which are specially recommended for younger learners. In addition to the introductions and activities in each Bookworm, resource material includes photocopiable test worksheets and Teacher's Handbooks, which contain advice on running a class library and using cassettes, and the answers for the activities in the books.

Several other series are linked to the OXFORD BOOKWORMS LIBRARY. They range from highly illustrated readers for young learners, to playscripts, non-fiction readers, and unsimplified texts for advanced learners.

Oxford Bookworms Starters   *Oxford Bookworms Factfiles*
Oxford Bookworms Playscripts *Oxford Bookworms Collection*

Details of these series and a full list of all titles in the OXFORD BOOKWORMS LIBRARY can be found in the *Oxford English* catalogues. A selection of titles from the OXFORD BOOKWORMS LIBRARY can be found on the next pages.

Cranford

ELIZABETH GASKELL

Retold by Kate Mattock

Life in the small English town of Cranford seems very quiet and peaceful. The ladies of Cranford lead tidy, regular lives. They make their visits between the hours of twelve and three, give little evening parties, and worry about their maid-servants. But life is not always smooth – there are little arguments and jealousies, sudden deaths and unexpected marriages . . .

Mrs Gaskell's timeless picture of small-town life in the first half of the nineteenth century has delighted readers for nearly 150 years.

Gulliver's Travels

JONATHAN SWIFT

Retold by Clare West

'Soon I felt something alive moving along my leg and up my body to my face, and when I looked down, I saw a very small human being, only fifteen centimetres tall . . . I was so surprised that I gave a great shout.'

But that is only the first of many surprises which Gulliver has on his travels. He visits a land of giants and a flying island, meets ghosts from the past and horses which talk . . .

BOOKWORMS • CLASSICS • STAGE 4

Washington Square

HENRY JAMES

Retold by Kieran McGovern

When a handsome young man begins to court Catherine Sloper, she feels she is very lucky. She is a quiet, gentle girl, but neither beautiful nor clever; no one had ever admired her before, or come to the front parlour of her home in Washington Square to whisper soft words of love to her.

But in New York in the 1840s young ladies are not free to marry where they please. Catherine must have her father's permission, and Dr Sloper is a rich man. One day Catherine will have a fortune of 30,000 dollars a year . . .

BOOKWORMS • THRILLER & ADVENTURE • STAGE 4

Mr Midshipman Hornblower

C. S. FORESTER

Retold by Rosemary Border

Hornblower fired. There was a small cloud of smoke, but no bang. 'This is death,' he thought. 'My pistol was the unloaded one.'

But Horatio Hornblower does not die. He survives the duel with Simpson, learns to overcome his seasickness, and goes on to risk his life many times over. It is 1793, Britain is at war with France, and life on a sailing ship of war is hard and dangerous. But the hardest battles are fought by Hornblower within himself.

BOOKWORMS · THRILLER & ADVENTURE · STAGE 4

We Didn't Mean to Go to Sea

ARTHUR RANSOME

Retold by Ralph Mowat

The four Walker children never meant to go to sea. They had promised their mother they would stay safely in the harbour, and would be home on Friday in time for tea.

But there they are in someone else's boat, drifting out to sea in a thick fog. When the fog lifts, they can turn round and sail back to the harbour. But then comes the wind and the storm, driving them out even further across the cold North Sea . . .

BOOKWORMS · HUMAN INTEREST · STAGE 5

Jeeves and Friends

P. G. WODEHOUSE

Retold by Clare West

What on earth would Bertie Wooster do without Jeeves, his valet? Jeeves is calm, tactful, resourceful, and has the answer to every problem. Bertie, a pleasant young man but a bit short of brains, turns to Jeeves every time he gets into trouble. And Bertie is *always* in trouble.

These six stories include the most famous of P. G. Wodehouse's memorable characters. There are three stories about Bertie and Jeeves, and three about Lord Emsworth, who, like Bertie, is often in trouble, battling with his fierce sister Lady Constance, and his even fiercer Scottish gardener, the red-bearded Angus McAllister . . .